SHERLOCK HOLMES'

Mini-Mysteries

Tom Bullimore

Illustrated by Ian Anderson

Sterling Publishing Co., Inc.
New York

Library of Congress Cataloging-in-Publication Data Available

2 4 6 8 10 9 7 5 3

Published by Sterling Publishing Co., Inc.
387 Park Avenue South, New York, NY 10016
© 2005 by Tom Bullimore
Distributed in Canada by Sterling Publishing
ᶜ/o Canadian Manda Group, 165 Dufferin Street
Toronto, Ontario, Canada M6K 3H6
Distributed in the United Kingdom by GMC Distribution Services
Castle Place, 166 High Street, Lewes, East Sussex, England BN7 1XU
Distributed in Australia by Capricorn Link (Australia) Pty. Ltd.
P.O. Box 704, Windsor, NSW 2756, Australia

Sterling ISBN 13: 978-1-4027-2653-8
ISBN 10: 1-4027-2653-8

For information about custom editions, special sales,
premium and corporate purchases, please contact
Sterling Special Sales Department at
800-805-5489 or specialsales@sterlingpub.com.

CONTENTS

Sherlock Holmes had been called to a high class casino where a murder had taken place. The great detective stood over the body of the victim and noted that a number of chips were scattered on the floor. In total there were 124 chips. If there were twice as many black chips as there were blue, and 6 more red chips than there were blue, and 6 less white chips than there were blue, how many chips of each color were on the floor?

Answer on page 105

Doctor Watson leaped aboard a hansom cab and found a wallet lying at his feet as he sat down. In the wallet was a total of £240 made up of £1, £5, and £10 notes. If there were exactly the same number of notes for each of the three denominations, how many notes were there in total?

Answer on page 105

Sherlock Holmes and Doctor Watson entered the annual Scotland Yard golf championship and both performed well, with Holmes finishing ahead of Watson in the top five. Holmes finished in front of Constable White but behind Sergeant Black, who finished ahead of Lestrade, and Watson finished in front of Constable White but behind Inspector Lestrade, who finished in front of Holmes. Can you give the order that the top five finished in?

Answer on page 105

Doctor Watson noticed the words PIPERS HEAVEN written on the wall outside the London College of Music and pointed them out to Sherlock Holmes. Holmes immediately asked Watson to rearrange the letters to form one twelve-lettered word. Can you do it?

Answer on page 105

Doctor Watson had just received his army pension. From the total he paid $^1/_6$ to Mrs. Hudson for services rendered, he paid for rent on his apartment, and of the remainder he placed fi in his bank account, and the remaining £61.50 in a box under his bed. Can you deduce just how much the good doctor had received for his army pension?

Answer on page 105

Sherlock Holmes and Doctor Watson were standing in the shadows of a large warehouse on the dockside of Tilbury Docks waiting for the illegal transfer of some goods from a ship. It had been a long and boring wait so far and to relieve the boredom Holmes pointed toward the ship and said, "Note the rope ladder hanging from the ship, Watson. There are 12 rungs showing above the water. The bottom rung is level with the water and each rung is 10 inches apart. The tide is rising and it will rise 3 more feet to the high tide mark. How many rungs will be exposed at the high tide mark?"

Watson, as usual, got the answer wrong. Can you do any better?

Answer on page 105

Holmes drew out a grid with 8 numbers on it, he then handed Watson three darts and asked him to score 20 with the three darts. Watson made several feeble attempts but never came close. Holmes then asked Watson to mentally calculate how many different ways there were of scoring 20 using all three darts. Once a combination of numbers has been used it can be used again in a different order. Can you come up with the answer?

$$10 \quad 9 \quad 8 \quad 7$$
$$6 \quad 5 \quad 4 \quad 3$$

Answer on page 105

Sherlock billed three clients for work he had carried out on their behalf. The combined total of the three bills was £130. If bill #1 was £20 more than bill #2, and bill #2 was £5 less than bill #3, can you work out the total of each individual bill?

Answer on page 105

While on holiday in the countryside, Sherlock Holmes found his break away from crime fighting interrupted when he chased after a criminal who had just robbed a local shop. The criminal, aware of Holmes's pursuit, took what he thought was a shortcut through a farmer's field. As he ran he spotted a large bull take over from Holmes in the chase. The criminal's speed increased to 48 miles per hour as he attempted to escape the mad bull. There was a look of horror on the criminal's face when he noticed the twenty-foot fence in front of him. Quickly he did a U-turn, passing the bull. On his way back the robber's average speed was 32 miles per hour. The bull's average speed was 40 miles per hour. The question is, did the bull catch him or did he reach the relative safety of the waiting detective in time?

Answer on page 105

Sherlock Holmes decided to call upon a lady who owned an antique shop that the duo believed was involved in some rather shady deals. When they arrived at the shop they found it closed with a sign hanging on the front door. The sign read: HER RIPE VICES.

What does it mean, Holmes?" asked Watson.

"Rearrange the letters to form one word, Watson," Holmes replied.

Can you do it?

Answer on page 105

While working on a case with Inspector Lestrade, Sherlock Holmes and Doctor Watson came across a large box of stolen coins. Watson opened the box and declared, "Great Scot, there must be 1,000 coins in here!"

Lestrade guessed that there was more like 1,100, while Holmes estimated that it was close to 950. If one was off by 65, another by 85, and the third by 35, how many coins were in the box?

Answer on page 105

"Take these letters, Watson: PPOROOFR. Now I want you to form the word PROOF as many times as you can. You can use each letter more than once but you cannot use the same combination of letters more than once." (Example: Use the first P, the first R, the first two O's, and the F. This combination cannot be made again by simply swapping the positions of the two O's.) Can you do it?

Answer on page 105

tor Watson obtained a warrant
ial's flat for stolen goods. In
ound a number of dominoes
l rather strange. There were
ominoes with 10 spots, domi-
iinoes with 6 spots. Altogether
its. If there was an equal num-
oes, just how many dominoes

Answer on page 105

In an attempt to track down a bank robber, Sherlock Holmes found himself visiting five London train stations within the space of a few hours. If he visited Euston after Waterloo but before Fenchurch, and visited Victoria after King's Cross but before Fenchurch, can you work out which station he went to last?

Answer on page 105

Mrs. Hudson had laid out five ties on Sherlock Holmes's bed to allow him to make his own choice on the one he preferred to wear for dinner that evening. From the following information can you deduce the order (from left to right) in which the ties were laid out?

The green tie was to the left of both the gray and the red ties. The blue tie was to the left of the green and the brown. The red tie was to the right of the brown, while the brown was to the right of the gray.

Answer on page 105

Sherlock Holmes was interviewing a shopkeeper about a recent robbery that had occurred at his shop. The shopkeeper was able to give Holmes the following information about the three robbers. Can you match up the correct information to each of them?

1. Jackson wore black shoes but he didn't have a scar on his left cheek.

2. The one with a tattoo on his hand wasn't named Pratchett nor did he have gray hair.

3. The one wearing brown shoes was bald.

4. Simpson had fair hair but he wasn't the one with a limp.

Answer on page 106

While traveling by hansom cab to Scotland Yard, Sherlock Holmes gave Watson the following sequence of letters and asked him to identify the next letter in the sequence. The sequence read:

Y, Y, H, L, Y, E, Y, T.

Watson claimed that it could take him months to work it out. Perhaps you can do better?

Answer on page106

Doctor Watson's sister was about to visit him at Baker Street and he asked Mrs. Hudson if she could prepare a special lunch. Mrs. Hudson was delighted to help and remarked that she didn't know that Watson had a sister. Watson informed Mrs. Hudson that his sister had three daughters of her own and that each of her daughters had three daughters. From this information can you deduce how many pairs of sisters are involved in Watson's statement?

Answer on page 106

Holmes set Watson the following word problem, which the good doctor solved in seven minutes flat. Can you do better? Insert two vowels into each of the following groups of letters to form a perfectly good word in each case: LGHTR, THMBL, PYRMD, NSWR.

Answer on page 106

Three robbers, aware that Sherlock Holmes was on their trail, quickly split up the proceeds from a robbery and went their separate ways. The money from the robbery totaled £1,101. If Carstairs had £6 more than Blyth, while Blyth had £10 more than Brook, how much did each of the three robbers end up with?

Answer on page 106

Sherlock Holmes and Doctor Watson were sitting in a quiet restaurant enjoying an evening meal when Watson took a sip of the house wine. "Great Scot, Holmes! This is ghastly...it tastes more like beer than wine!" the good doctor exclaimed.

"I fear you exaggerate, Watson," replied Holmes. "But can you change the word WINE into BEER, by changing one letter at a time, and always creating a new, good English word?"

Watson achieved it in six steps. Can you do the same, or better?

Answer on page 106

A friend of Sherlock Holmes, Sir Reginald Grimsby, gave away £3,395 to children at the local poorhouse. Each child received the same amount (in full pounds). If there were less than 100 children but more than 50, can you deduce how much each of them received?

Answer on page 106

"I think I'll take a walk down to the tavern, Watson, and partake in a small refreshment," said Holmes. "Do you wish to join me?" he added.

"It's a cold night, Holmes," replied Watson. "Let me get my winter coat."

"Interesting reply," said Holmes. "If you take the words, WINTER COAT, and rearrange the letters you can form a refreshment."

Can you do it?

Answer on page 106

Sherlock Holmes stopped at a street corner to talk to a flower seller. The old lady was selling single white roses and red roses. Holmes discovered that she had sold 120 roses that day and had made £6. Of the 120 roses sold, only ¼ of them were white. If the red roses were sold at three times the price of the white roses, how much did a red rose cost?

Answer on page 106

Doctor Watson was moving to his new apartment on Baker Street with the assistance of his good friend Sherlock Holmes. Watson had nine large boxes to transport. Each box was numbered 1 through 9 and stacked in three rows (see diagram). Holmes noted that no box had a smaller numbered box than its own below it or to the right of it, which prompted Holmes to ask the good doctor the following question. "How many different ways in total could the boxes be arranged keeping to the formula of no smaller number below it or to the right of it?"

Needless to say Doctor Watson could not supply the answer. Perhaps you can.

ARRANGEMENT OF BOXES

1	2	3
4	5	6
7	8	9

Answer on page 106

Sherlock Holmes was hot on the trail of a band of twelve criminals who were carrying out robberies in South London. The band consisted of nine men and three women and, aware that Holmes was hot on their trail, they had decided to leave London and go their separate ways. Before they went they agreed to share equally the money they each possessed. If every male criminal gave an equal amount to each of the female criminals, and every female gave an equal amount to each of the males, so that each of the twelve now had exactly the same amount, can you deduce the smallest possible (in full pounds) amount each possessed?

Answer on page 106

Sherlock Holmes spent a total of £1000 on one hundred items at an antique shop. Holmes only bought three different types of items: gold coins at £50 each, books at £10 each and pipes at 50 pence each. Can you work out how many of each he bought?

Answer on page 106

Sherlock Holmes, Doctor Watson, and Inspector Lestrade took a journey of 40 miles in total. Watson walked at 1 mile per hour, Lestrade walked at 2 miles per hour, while Holmes (being smart as usual) traveled by hansom cab at 8 miles per hour. Holmes took Watson a certain distance in the cab and dropped him off to walk the remainder. He then drove back until he picked up Lestrade and took him to their destination, where all three arrived at the same time. Can you work out how long the journey took?

Answer on page 106

Sherlock Holmes was strolling in Hyde Park when he glanced around and saw his good friend Doctor Watson exactly 400 yards behind him and walking toward him. They then each walked 200 yards in a direct line, facing each other, at which time you would have thought they would have met. Yet it was not the case, in fact, they were still 400 yards apart. How can this be?

Answer on page 107

From a ship berthed at London Docks, Sherlock Holmes bought two types of pipe tobacco: one at 32 pence per pound, and the other at 40 pence a pound. Holmes then mixed together some of each, which he proposed to sell at his club for 43 pence a pound and make a profit of 25% on the cost. How many pounds of each kind must he use to make a mixture of 100 pounds in weight?

Answer on page 107

A workman was digging a hole outside 221b Baker Street as Sherlock Holmes walked by. "How deep is that hole?" asked Holmes, when he had the attention of the workman.

"Take a guess, Guv," replied the workman. "I'm exactly five feet ten inches tall," he added.

"How much deeper are you going?" asked Holmes.

"Twice as deep," he replied. "Then my head will be twice as far below ground as it is above ground now." From this information Holmes was able to deduce how deep the hole would be when the workman had finished. Can you?

Answer on page 107

35

Sherlock Holmes was sitting by the fire reading when Doctor Watson entered the study. "Who are you reading now, Holmes?" asked Watson.

"Our greatest novelist, señor!" replied Holmes.

"What's with this 'señor' business?" inquired Watson.

Holmes sighed, "You asked a question, Watson, and I answered. If you were to rearrange all the letters of my answer you could reveal the author of the book I'm reading."

The task was above Watson, can you do it?

Answer on page 107

Sherlock Holmes was about to start a round of golf on a nine-hole golf course with Doctor Watson as his playing partner. First, Holmes studied the distances of each hole (see golf card below), then asked Watson the following question: "Assuming, Watson, that I could always strike the ball in a perfectly straight line and send it exactly one of two distances, what would be the two distances that would take me around in the least number of strokes?"

The question only served to put Watson off his game and he had a terrible round of golf. Perhaps you can come up with the answer?

1	300 yds
2	250 yds
3	200 yds
4	325 yds
5	275 yds
6	350 yds
7	225 yds
8	375 yds
9	400 yds

Answer on page 107

Holmes and Watson sat by a roaring fire on a winter's night enjoying a nightcap before retiring when Holmes asked Watson to write down 5 odd numbers that would add up to 14. Needless to say Watson didn't achieve it and went off to bed in a huff. Can you do it?

Answer on page 107

Sherlock Holmes sat in the courtroom where three prisoners stood in the dock. Holmes had been responsible for the arrest of all three and was following the proceedings with some interest. In the dock, Montgomery stood between a man who was clean shaven and a man who stole a cigar case. Walton, who stole a wallet, had been caught by Holmes along with Murphy. The man with the mustache—not the one with the beard—had stolen a gold watch. From this information can you identify each man, indicating whether he was clean shaven, had a beard or a mustache, and the item each was accused of stealing?

Answer on page 107

During a murder inquiry, Holmes interviewed three suspects: Messrs. Smith, Granger, and Lyle. Their occupations were that of doctor, carpenter, and blacksmith. From the interviews, Holmes was given the following facts: Lyle is not the blacksmith. Smith is not the carpenter. Lyle is the carpenter. Smith is not the blacksmith. Holmes soon discovered that of these four facts only one of them was true. He was then able to deduce the true occupation of each of the four men. Can you?

Answer on page 107

Sherlock Holmes, Doctor Watson, and Inspector Lestrade were sitting by a roaring fire one New Year's eve discussing their arrests during the previous twelve months. They had made a total of 119 arrests between them. If Holmes had made 11 more arrests than Lestrade, and Lestrade 9 more than Watson, can you deduce how many arrests they had each made?

Answer on page 107

A blind matchstick seller was standing on a street corner when three youths approached. The first youth picked up fi the boxes of matches in the matchstick seller's tray, but then returned 10 of the boxes. The second youth took ⅓ of the boxes that remained, but then returned 2 of the boxes. The third youth took ½ of the remaining boxes, but then returned 1, leaving 12 boxes in the tray. Can you deduce how many boxes the seller originally had in the tray? (Incidentally the three youths did not get away with the crime. The matchstick seller just happened to be Sherlock Holmes in disguise.)

Answer on page 107

At a meeting at the Criminologists' Club, a number of the members walked out in disagreement over a certain issue. The secretary of the club commented to Holmes that he had thought about leaving himself, which would have meant that ⅔ of the members would have left. Holmes agreed but pointed out that he could persuade Doctor Watson and Inspector Lestrade to return, which would mean only ½ the members would be missing. Can you deduce just how many members were originally present at the meeting?

Answer on page 107

Five petty criminals, unaware that they were being observed by Sherlock Holmes, sat in the corner of a tavern counting out their takings for the day. In total they had £70 between them. From the following information can you work out just exactly how much each man had?

White had £3 more than Black, Gray had £3 more than White, Brown had £6 more than White, while Green had £12 more than Black.

Answer on page 107

Mrs. Hudson, the housekeeper at 221b Baker Street, had baked some fairy cakes (they were Watson's favorites) and some apple tarts. The combined total of the tarts and cakes was 41. If there were 5 more tarts than there were fairy cakes, how many did she bake of each?

Answer on page 107

Doctor Watson opened up his piggy bank and counted out the contents. He discovered he had a total of £3.78, made up of 1p, 2p, 5p and 10p coins. Watson then discovered that he had exactly the same amount of coins for each denomination. Can you deduce how many coins Watson had in his piggy bank in total?

Answer on page 107

Sherlock Holmes traced a number of stolen silver candlesticks to an antique dealer in South London. The dealer admitted buying the candlesticks at a cost of £150, but that he only had 8 left having sold the remainder for £121 and making 50p on each of them. How many candlesticks did the dealer buy in the first place?

Answer on page 107

Sherlock Holmes and Doctor Watson visited a fairground where Watson couldn't resist having a go on a rifle stall. Watson claimed to the stall owner that he could hit the bull's-eye on each occasion, firing a shot a minute. The stall owner said that he would hand over his star prize if Watson succeeded. Exactly one hour had elapsed when the good doctor's 60th shot hit the bull's-eye and he claimed his prize. The stall owner refused to pay up on the grounds that the doctor had gone over the time limit. Was the stall owner correct?

Answer on page 108

Sherlock Holmes and Doctor Watson retrieved the money stolen from Lord Melley's private safe. They found the £5000 buried in the grounds of his lordship's expansive estate. On finding the money, Holmes and Watson returned to Lord Melley's residence and took on the task of counting the money to ensure it was all there, which it was. If Watson's pile of banknotes totaled £1002 more than those counted by Holmes, how much money did Holmes have in his pile?

Answer on page 108

Five criminals, hotly pursued by Sherlock Holmes, had left the scene of a crime and were running toward Tilbury Docks. Wilkins did not arrive at the docks first and Jenkins was neither first nor last, while Tomkins arrived directly behind Wilkins, Jackson didn't arrive second, and Morton arrived two places behind Jackson. Can you deduce the order in which the men arrived at the docks?

Answer on page 108

Sherlock Holmes was spending a weekend in the country, training for the London Marathon. If the great detective had cut down his pipe smoking by a third in order to get fit, how far could he run into a forest during a training stint?

Answer on page 108

Sherlock Holmes sat in his club awaiting the arrival of Doctor Watson.

"Ah Watson," said Holmes, when the good doctor appeared. "While I was waiting for you, I passed the time by tossing this coin in the air. It came up heads on each of the ten occasions. Can you tell me what the probability is that it will come up heads on the eleventh toss?" Can you supply Holmes with the answer?

Answer on page 108

Doctor Watson handed his loose change to one of the Baker Street Irregulars who was standing outside 22lb Baker Street. It transpired that Watson had £3.34p in change, made up of 1p, 2p, 5p and 10p coins. If the good doctor had exactly the same number of each denomination, can you deduce how many coins he gave away in total?

Answer on page 108

Sherlock Holmes interviewed five prisoners who were in five different cells at Scotland Yard. The cells were numbered from left to right, 1 through 5. From the following information, can you deduce which prisoner was in which cell?

1. Forrest was in the cell to the right of Medwin but to the left of Gould.

2. Allison was in the cell to the right of Gould but to the left of Mercer.

Answer on page 108

Sherlock Holmes dealt out five playing cards face up on a table. If the queen of hearts was directly to the right of the 9 of clubs, while the 4 of diamonds was to the right of the 3 of hearts but to the left of the 2 of spades, and the 2 of spades was directly to the right of the queen of hearts, while the club had a red card on either side of it, can you determine the row of cards as they read from left to right?

Answer on page 108

Sherlock Holmes, Doctor Watson, Sergeant Black, and Inspector Lestrade were all prosecuting witnesses at a murder trial. From the following information can you deduce in which order they were called in to give their evidence?

1. Holmes was called to the dock after Sgt. Black but before Watson.

2. Lestrade was called before Holmes but after Sgt. Black.

Answer on page 108

"Take these two words, Watson, EVEN GAIT," said Holmes, "and rearrange them to form one good eight-lettered word."

Watson, at his normal swift speed, solved the problem just before darkness set in. Can you do better?

Answer on page 108

For a forthcoming weekend in the countryside, Sherlock purchased a pair of hiking boots, a deerstalker, and a walking cane for a total of £11.50. If the deerstalker cost half the price of the hiking boots, and the walking cane cost ⅟₇ of the price paid for the hiking boots, how much did Holmes pay for each of the three items?

Answer on page 108

On a cold winter's night, Sherlock Holmes and Doctor Watson sat by a roaring fire in the study of 221b Baker Street. "Amuse your mind with this puzzler, Watson," said Holmes, breaking the silence that had existed between them for some time. "Take these four numbers: 701, 1095, 1417, and 2312. Now divide them by the largest number possible that will leave the same remainder in each case." Watson spent over an hour scribbling away on a notepad but with little success. Perhaps you can do better?

Answer on page 108

NUMBER CRUNCHING

Sherlock Holmes drew out the following box and asked Watson to fill in the missing number. Watson took seven minutes to come up with the correct answer. Can you do better?

$$
\begin{array}{cccc}
2 & 3 & 5 & 4 \\
1 & 4 & 6 & 3 \\
5 & 5 & 2 & ? \\
4 & 6 & 3 & 1
\end{array}
$$

Answer on page 108

Doctor Watson and Sergeant Black, working under the instructions of Sherlock Holmes, were visiting every household in Green Street making inquiries into a recent murder that had taken place in the vicinity. Watson arrived in the street first and had called on three houses on the south side when Sergeant Black arrived and informed Watson that it was he who had been instructed to call on the south side. Watson mumbled to himself and set off to work on the north side while the sergeant continued where Watson had left off. When the sergeant had completed his side of the street he crossed over and called on six houses on Watson's side before the street was complete. As there were an equal number of houses on each side of the street, can you determine which of the two men called on the most houses and by how many?

Answer on page 109

Inspector Lestrade was explaining to Doctor Watson that he lived in a street with more than twenty houses but fewer than five hundred. He further explained that all the houses were numbered 1, 2, 3, 4, 5, etc. up to the last number of the last house. If all the numbers from 1 to the number of Lestrade's house added up to exactly half the sum of all the numbers from 1 up to and including the last house, can you deduce the number of Inspector Lestrade's house?

Answer on page 109

Sherlock Holmes was interviewing two criminals in Inspector Lestrade's office at Scotland Yard. He asked each his age and then asked each of them to add their two ages together. One gave an answer of 21 while the other gave an answer of 646. Holmes quickly realized that the first criminal had subtracted one age from the other, while the second had multiplied them together. Can you work out the ages of the two criminals?

Answer on page 109

"What's this, Holmes?" asked Inspector Lestrade as Sherlock Holmes placed five leather bags on the inspector's desk. "It's the missing 178 diamonds," replied Holmes. In the first and second bags there were a total of 65 diamonds, in the second and third were 69, while in the third and fourth there were 73, and in the fourth and fifth were 71. How many diamonds were in each of the five bags?

Answer on page 109

"Here's a puzzler for you, Watson," said Sherlock Holmes. "What number can be multiplied by either one, two, three, four, five or six, where no new figure appears in the answer?" Watson gave up after ten minutes, perhaps you can do better?

Answer on page 109

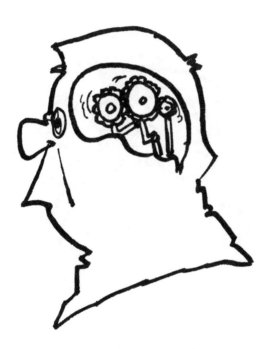

Sherlock Holmes arrested three pickpockets at Waterloo Station who, between them, had a total of £23. If Fingers had £2 more than Shifty but £6 less than Knuckles, how much did each of the three pickpockets have in their possession?

Answer on page 109

Sherlock Holmes uncovered a series of robberies that had been carried out in the vicinity of the London docks. Three dock workers were involved in a total of 36 crimes. Kipper took part in five less robberies than Haddock, who in turn took part in five less crimes than Halibut. From this information can you deduce the number of crimes each of the three men took part in?

Answer on page 109

In the Gallery of the Central Criminal Court there are four seats in a row. Holmes is sitting next to Watson, but not next to Lestrade. Lestrade isn't sitting next to Sergeant Black. From this can you deduce who is sitting next to the Sergeant?

Answer on page 109

65

Sherlock Holmes decided to sell off his collection of antique pipes and took out an advertisement in the Times announcing the fact. To the first interested caller at 221b Baker Street, he sold ½ his collection plus ½ a pipe. To the second he sold ½ of what remained plus ½ a pipe. To the third caller he sold ½ of what remained plus ½ a pipe, which left the master detective with no antique pipes. If each caller received whole pipes only, how many antique pipes did Holmes have for sale in the first place?

Answer on page 109

65

Sherlock Holmes decided to sell off his collection of antique pipes and took out an advertisement in the Times announcing the fact. To the first interested caller at 221b Baker Street, he sold ½ his collection plus ½ a pipe. To the second he sold ½ of what remained plus ½ a pipe. To the third caller he sold ½ of what remained plus ½ a pipe, which left the master detective with no antique pipes. If each caller received whole pipes only, how many antique pipes did Holmes have for sale in the first place?

Answer on page 109

Sherlock Holmes and Doctor Watson were doing their Christmas shopping together. They had a total of £84 between them to spend, with Holmes having £12 more than Watson. If Watson spent ¾ of his total, leaving him with £6 more than Holmes was left with, how much did Holmes spend?

Answer on page 109

Sherlock Holmes glanced up from reading his newspaper and said, "Watson, what is the only word that when you add additional letters, becomes smaller?"

Watson simply stared at the great detective with utter confusion on his face. I'm sure you can do better.

Answer on page 109

"What are you reading now, Watson?" asked Holmes as he entered the study of 221b Baker Street.

"The Bible, Holmes," Watson replied.

"Then tell me, Watson, how many pairs of animals did Moses count as they came off the Ark?" Watson answered incorrectly on every attempt. Can you do better?

Answer on page 109

Sherlock Holmes pointd out the following strange signpost for Doctor Watson. Can you work out how the distances are achieved and therefore reveal the miles to Dundee?

BRIGHTON 36
ALDERSHOT 42
DUNDEE ?

Answer on page 109

Sherlock Holmes drew out the following magic square where the three columns, the three rows, and the two diagonals add up to the same total. In the total square, he uses only four numbers: 1, 2, 3, and 4 (using each of the numbers nine times). He then asks his colleague, Doctor Watson, to use nine different four-digit numbers, using the same numbers: 1, 2, 3, and 4 (nine times each) to make another perfect magic square. Watson was having great difficulty, so the great detective gave him a clue by supplying him with the center number, 2242. Watson was then able to complete the square in twenty minutes—can you beat Watson's time?

1234   1234   1234
1234   1234   1234
1234   1234   1234

Answer on page 109

Sherlock Holmes took a hansom cab from Baker Street that cost him half the money he had in his pocket. On arriving at his destination he purchased a magazine for 25p from a street seller. He then sat in a café having tea and crumpets, which cost him half of his remaining money plus 2 and half pence. Holmes then entered a tobacconist's where he bought some pipe tobacco at a cost of 50p. At this point Holmes noted that he had exactly 10p left. Can you work out how much the great detective had to begin with?

Answer on page 109

Sherlock Holmes, Doctor Watson, and Inspector Lestrade were interviewing a known informant. They were seeking information on a recent robbery. The informant told them he could supply the names of the two robbers at a price of £25. The three of them quickly emptied their pockets and thankfully discovered that the amount asked for by the informant was exactly the amount of money they had between them. If Holmes had £2 more than Lestrade but £3 less than Watson, can you work out how much money each of them possessed?

Answer on page 110

Doctor Watson had three medical books in his apartment standing side by side. The books, placed in order: volumes 1, 2, and 3 were each exactly one-inch thick. A bookworm went to work outside the front cover of volume 1 and began to eat its way through to the outside of the back cover of volume 3. If the worm travels in a straight line, how far does it travel?

Answer on page 110

BURP!

Sherlock Holmes and Doctor Watson were playing a card game with a stake of one penny per game. When they finished playing Holmes had won three games and the other had won three pennies. How many games had they actually played?

Answer on page 110

Sherlock Holmes gave Watson the following puzzler to work out involving a number with three digits; 9, 5, and one other. He told Watson if these digits are reversed and then subtracted from the original number the answer will contain the same three digits in a different order still. Can you work out what the third digit is?

Answer on page 110

An old friend of Sherlock Holmes had lived a ¼ of his life as a boy, ⅕ of his life as a young man, ⅓ of his life in the army, and 13 years on an army pension. How old is Holmes's friend now?

Answer on page 110

Sherlock Holmes and Doctor Watson went on a much deserved holiday. During the holiday it rained on 13 days, but when it rained in the morning, the afternoon was fine, and every rainy afternoon was preceded by a fine morning. There were 11 fine mornings and 12 fine afternoons. How long was their holiday?

Answer on page 110

Doctor Watson bought a large bottle of ginger beer which cost him 24 pence. The ginger beer cost 12 pence more than the bottle. How much should Watson receive on returning the bottle?

Answer on page 110

If Sherlock Holmes hired five of the Baker Street Irregulars to pack boxes of garden trash and they packed 5 boxes in five minutes, how many irregulars would he need to pack 50 boxes in 50 minutes?

Answer on page 110

Professor Moriarty and a few of his accomplices were removing a safe from an office by using two cylindrical steel bars, both 7 inches in diameter, as rollers. How far will the safe have moved forward when the rollers have made one revolution?

Answer on page 110

81

Sherlock Holmes caught one fish during his fishing trip with Doctor Watson. The fish had a tail as long as its head plus ¼ the length of its body. Its body was ¾ of its total length. Its head was 4 inches long. What was the length of the fish caught by Holmes?

Answer on page 110

During a game of billiards, Holmes can give Watson 10 points in 50, and Watson can give Inspector Lestrade 10 points in 50. How many points can Holmes give Lestrade to make it an even game?

Answer on page 110

Sherlock Holmes and Doctor Watson were given £100 in the will of an old client. If ⅓ of Holmes's portion was deducted from ¼ of Watson's, the remainder would be £11. What was the amount that each were left in the legacy?

Answer on page 110

Sherlock Holmes apprehended three pickpockets who had a total of £65 between them. If Anderson had £5 less than Bradford, and Collins had £4 more than Bradford, how much money did each of the three men have in their possession?

Answer on page 110

Sherlock Holmes gave away £3,395 to his favorite charities at Christmas time. If there were more than fifty charities involved but less than one hundred, and each charity received exactly the same amount in whole pounds only, how many charities were there and how much did they each receive?

Answer on page 110

Following several recent attempts by robbers to break into his home at 221b Baker Street, Sherlock Holmes purchased a large guard dog, only to find it was friendly with anyone who entered the house. Lord Brown, a friend of the great detective, grew fond of the dog and bought the animal from Holmes. Holmes sold the dog for £35, plus half as much as he had paid for it. If Holmes made a profit of £10.50, how much did he originally pay for the dog?

Answer on page 110

In an effort to test the mind of his colleague Doctor Watson, Sherlock Holmes set the following puzzler with the use of dominoes. He then asked Watson to arrange the dominoes in such a way that all four sides of the rectangle contain the same number of pips. The six dominoes used are: double blank, 1/1, 2/2, 0/2, 0/1, and 1/2. Can you do it?

Answer on page 110

At a fair, Sherlock Holmes was introduced by Inspector Lestrade to a colleague of his from Scotland Yard. The gentleman had his two sons, John and Paul, by his side. Holmes learned that the two boys were born on the same day of the same year and were the children of the same parents yet they were not twins. How can this be?

Answer on page 111

Lord Brimestone was found drowned in his own garden pool. Sherlock Holmes was immediately called to the scene. Holmes questioned the butler, gardener, and the footman. They each said the following:

1. The butler: "If it was murder, the footman did it."

2. The footman: "If it was murder, I did not do it."

3. The gardener: "If it was not murder, it was suicide."

Sherlock Holmes said correctly to Watson, "If just one of these three men lied, it was suicide."

Can you deduce whether it was a murder, an accident, or a suicide?

Answer on page 111

Sherlock Holmes gave his colleague Doctor Watson the following puzzler to work on: Using the following numbers in the order that they are presented, he asked Watson to insert the mathematical signs required to produce the answer of 6. Can you do it? The numbers were: 3, 7, 9, 6, 8, 4.

Answer on page 111

Sherlock Holmes went to his local tobacco shop to purchase a pouch of pipe tobacco. As he waited to get served he noticed a new brand of Dutch tobacco on the shelf and decided to buy a pack to give it a try. The tobacconist told Holmes that it had been a busy day for pipe tobacco, having sold 99 pouches in all. If the tobacconist had earned £33 from pipe tobacco during the day, and ⅓ of the tobacco sold was Dutch at the cost of 3 times the price of the ordinary tobacco, how much did a pouch of Dutch tobacco cost?

Answer on page 111

Sherlock Holmes handed Watson a 5-pint container and a 3-pint container, and asked him to measure out 1 pint of water. Assuming Watson had an endless supply of water can you find the quickest way to do this?

Answer on page 111

Sherlock Holmes apprehended two pickpockets who turned out to be brothers. The combined total of their ages was 48 years. Holmes had previously arrested both of them some 8 years ago when the youngest of the two was ¼ the age of his brother. How old were they both now?

Answer on page 111

Sherlock Holmes asked his good friend Doctor Watson to provide him with a 16-lettered word in which the only vowel is the letter E, which is used 3 times in the word. Watson failed, perhaps you can do better?

Answer on page 111

As they sat enjoying a late night drink in the study of 221b Baker Street, Sherlock Holmes and Doctor Watson tested each other with a few tricky puzzlers.

"Try this one," said Holmes. "If we were both to start off from the same point and you walked due north and covered 7 miles a day, while I walked due south and covered 11 miles a day, how much distance would be between us on the twelfth day following our departure?"

Answer on page 111

A good friend of Sherlock Holmes' asked the great detective how many murder cases he had worked on during the year. Holmes replied, "If I had worked on as many again, plus ½ as many, and ¼ as many, I would have worked on 99 cases."

Can you work out how many murder cases Holmes had actually worked on?

Answer on page 111

"Take the words, NEW DOOR, now rearrange the letters, Watson, and make one word," said Sherlock Holmes to his colleague. Can you do it?

Answer on page 111

Sherlock Holmes told Doctor Watson that he could sit six people in a room all with their backs to the same wall, he could then place an apple in the room (the room would be completely void of furniture and any other obstacle) in such a way that only five of the six could see the apple. How could he do it?

Answer on page 111

Holmes placed a little wager with Doctor Watson that he could grip something with his left hand that the good doctor couldn't hold with his left hand. Watson took the wager and lost. What was it that Holmes held in his left hand?

Answer on page 111

"Imagine this," said Sherlock Holmes to his colleague Doctor Watson, "You are on one side of a river and I am on the other. We each have a motorboat and start off at exactly the same time en route to the opposite bank. We both travel at constant speeds throughout—although my boat travels faster than yours. We pass at a point 720 yards from the nearest bank. When we have both arrived at our respective banks, we begin the return journey. On the return we meet 400 yards from the other bank. The question is, Watson: How wide is the river?"

"Pardon?" said a confused Watson.

Perhaps you can supply the answer?

Answer on page 111

ANSWERS

1. 19 white, 25 blue, 30 red, 50 black.

2. 45 notes (15 of each)

3. 1. Sgt. Black 2. Lestrade 3. Holmes 4. Watson 5. White.

4. APPREHENSIVE

5. £246.

6. Still 12. (The ship and the ladder will rise with the tide.)

7. 48 ways.

8. 1. £55 2. £ 35 3. £40

9. The criminal's average speed was 38.4 mph, so the odds were in favor of the bull catching him.

10. RECEIVERSHIP

11. 1035

12. 24

13. 54 (nine of each)

14. Fenchurch

15. Blue, green, gray, brown, red

16. Pratchett: scar, brown shoes, bald; Jackson: limp, black shoes, gray hair; Simpson: tattoo, gray shoes, fair hair.

17. "R" (Each letter is the last letter of the months of the year.)

18. 12 pairs of sisters

19. LIGHTER. THIMBLE. PYRAMID. ANSWER.

20. BLYTH £355; BROOK £345; CARSTAIRS £401.

21. WINE, WIND, WEND, BEND, BEAD, BEAR, BEER.

22. £35 (97 children)

23. TONIC WATER

24. 6 pence

25. Including the arrangement as seen in the diagram, there are 42 different arrangements.

26. Every male starts with £3, and gives £1 to each female. Each female starts with £15 and gives £2 to every male. Each person then has £6.

27. 19 coins, 1 book, 80 pipes.

28. The journey took 10 hours. Watson walked 5 miles at the end of his journey. Lestrade walked 13 at the beginning and Holmes's hansom cab went a total of 80 miles.

29. One of them was walking backward.

30. 70 lb of the 32 pence tobacco and 30 lb of the 40 pence tobacco.

31. 10 feet 6 inches.

32. Robert Louis Stevenson

33. 26 strokes in all (two distances: 100 yards & 125 yards)

34. 11, 1, 1, 1.

35. Montgomery: mustache, gold watch; Murphy: beard, cigar case; Walton: clean shaven, wallet.

36. Smith—carpenter. Granger—doctor; Lyle—blacksmith.

37. Holmes, 50; Lestrade, 39; Watson, 30.

38. 40 boxes

39. 18

40. Black £8; White £11; Gray £14; Brown £17; Green £20.

41. 23 apple tarts, 18 fairy cakes.

42. 84 coins (21 of each denomination)

43. 30 (at a cost of £5 each)

44. Yes. (Watson should have taken 59 minutes to fire 60 shots. The time from the first shot to the second should only have been 1 minute.)

45. £1999

46. Jackson, Jenkins, Morton, Wilkins, Tomkins.

47. Halfway. (After that he would be running out of the forest.)

48. 50/50 (It is irrelevant what went on the previous throws.)

49. Watson gave away a total of 52 coins (13 of each denomination).

50. 1. Medwin 2. Forrest 3. Gould 4. Allison 5. Mercer

51. 3 of hearts, 4 of diamonds, 9 of clubs, queen of hearts, 2 of spades.

52. Sgt. Black, Lestrade, Holmes, Watson.

53. NEGATIVE

54. Walking stick, £1; deerstalker, £3.50; hiking boots, £7.

55. Divide by 179, which leaves 164 in each case.

56. 2 (In each horizontal column the first and the third numbers and the second and the fourth numbers combined totals 7.)

57. Sergeant Black called on six more houses than Watson.

58. 84 (there were 119 houses in total)

59. Their ages were 17 and 38.

60. 1st bag—38; 2nd—27; 3rd—42; 4th—>31; 5th—40.

61. 142,857

62. Fingers £7, Shifty £5, Knuckles £11.

63. Kipper, 7; Haddock, 12; Halibut, 17.

64. Holmes (seating: Black, Holmes, Watson, Lestrade).

65. 7 pipes

66. Holmes spent £45.

67. Small

68. None! (It was noah not moses.)

69. 30 miles to Dundee, (6 miles for each vowel and 4 for each consonant.)

70.

2243	1341	3142
3141	2242	1343
1342	3143	2241

71. £3

72. Lestrade, £6; Holmes, £8; Watson, £11.

73. 1 inch

74. Nine games

75. The number 4.

76. 60 years old

77. 18 days

78. 6 pence

79. The same: 5

80. 44 inches

81. 128 inches

82. 18 points

83. Holmes, £24; Watson, £76.

84. Anderson, £17; Bradford, £22; Collins, £26.

85. 97 Charities—each received 35 pounds.

86. £49

87. Dominoes top row from left to right: 0/1, 0/2; Left vertical: 2/2; Right vertical: 1/2; Bottom two from left to right: 0/0 1/1.

88. They were two children from a set of triplets.

89. It was suicide.

90. 3 x 7 - 9 + 6 - 8 - 4 = 6

91. 60p per pouch.

92. Fill the 3-pint container and empty it into the 5-pint container. Fill the 3-pint container again and empty it into the 5-pint container until full. 1 pint will now remain in the 3-pint container.

93. 32 years and 16 years.

94. STRENGTHLESSNESS

95. 216 miles

96. 36

97. ONE WORD

98. Place the apple on the person's head.

99. Watson's left elbow

100. 1 mile wide

INDEX